# PLAY FRESH

Keon Williams Jr.

WestBow Press books may be ordered through booksellers or by contacting:

WestBow Press
A Division of Thomas Nelson & Zondervan
1663 Liberty Drive
Bloomington, IN 47403
www.westbowpress.com
844-714-3454

Interior Image Credit: Elijah Pemberton

ISBN: 978-1-6642-5162-5 (sc)
ISBN: 978-1-6642-5163-2 (e)

Library of Congress Control Number: 2021929429

Print information available on the last page.

WestBow Press rev. date: 02/04/2022

WESTBOW
PRESS®
A DIVISION OF THOMAS NELSON
& ZONDERVAN

# Foreword:

Huddle up, readers, and help us kick off our journey with Team Green Machines versus Team Garbage Mites. Let's give a warm welcome to first-time author Keon Williams. Keon is a bond trader and an environmental activist. His environmentally savvy ways benefit our world. He is a believer in educating our youth so that they can take part in making our world a safe place for many years to come. I am proud to have been Keon's kindergarten teacher many years ago. I fondly remember Keon's drive and ambition to succeed in all he did as a kindergarten student. As an author, he is continuing to show his ambition and desire for success. His willingness to help educate others on ways to help make our world a healthy, safe world is admirable. Team Green Machines demonstrates Keon's view on environmental care. Using his witty ways, he takes his readers through two approaches to how people care for our world. He uses real-life experiences to give his readers a glimpse of how we can all help set our world on a healthy path. Keon uses comparison and contrast throughout his story, providing opportunities for higher-level thinking to his audience. He will have his readers thinking twice about what they do on a daily basis. Take this opportunity to let Keon Williams be your teacher on environmental care. I hope to have many more students just like Keon: smart, ambitious, caring, and eager to take care of the world we live in. It is my sincere pleasure to leave you in the pages of Keon Williams's thoughts.

Enjoy!
Melissa Hitzges

# Acknowledgment:

Jireh, LaTasha Pitts, Keon Williams Sr., Lauren Williams, Keyaira Williams, Cynthia Patterson, Jacqueline Lott, Savena Mushinge, Elijah Pemberton, Rena Patel, Frank Van Buren, Melissa Hitzges and Bill Miller

President Earth greeted the two teams at the entrance of Greentopia University. It was the day before the Garden Football League Championship, where only one team would emerge victorious.

First to arrive was Team Garbage Mites. They came to a screeching halt in front of the university, parked their oversized dump trucks over a flower bed, and wobbled over to the gate as the trucks let out their final **pssshhh** of pollution.

Moments later, Team Green Machines glided into the parking lot on their **electric bus**. They exited their vehicle carrying their neatly packed belongings and marched proudly up the walkway as their bus powered down silently.

3

"Welcome to Greentopia University!" called President Earth. "Here the grass is always green, the air is always clean, and the sun is always seen. Tomorrow morning, you will compete for the chance to be crowned Garden Football League Champions. Enjoy your stay, and please do your part to keep Greentopia **green, clean, and serene!**"

The teams immediately met with their coaches.

The Garbage Mites flocked to Coach Landfill, smashing cans and chanting, "Smash it! Stash it! Trash it!" They ran in clumsy circles, dropping litter as they practiced their skills.

The Green Machines shook Coach Lettuce's hand and chanted, **"Reduce! Reuse! Recycle!"** They sprinted up and down the field, fueling their bodies with fresh water and clean air as they completed drill after drill.

6

After practice time, the teams made their way to the snack bar.

The Garbage Mites ate extra greasy deep-fried onion rings. They chowed down on gigantic double-wide donuts and drank sugary fruit juice. On their way out, they stashed sour gummies in their pockets. The Garbage Mites left their gummy wrappers and juice cans on the tables and in the grass where they'd eaten.

The Green Machines treated themselves to baked crackers and cheese sticks. They drank milk and enjoyed fresh fruit salad. As soon as they were done, they **recycled** their milk cartons.

Then the two teams went to bed.

The Garbage Mites burst into their rooms, jumped on the sofa, and yanked on the ceiling fan. They cranked up the air conditioning and kept the windows wide open. Then they turned on the TV and played video games until they fell asleep without even brushing their teeth.

When they finally woke up in the morning, they were **very groggy**. They all took **long showers** and brushed their teeth without shutting the faucet or letting the sink drain. Foamy toothpaste water overflowed the sink and got everywhere, and they did not bother to clean it.

The Green Machines walked quietly into their room and respectfully set down their things. They opened the windows and lifted the blinds in order to allow **fresh air** into their room.

All of them took **short showers** and brushed their teeth, remembering to shut the faucet off in between uses, and got into bed. When the sunlight filtered through the blinds the next morning, the Green Machines didn't even need to turn on the room lights.

The teams got dressed in their team uniforms and headed to brunch.

The Garbage Mites plopped themselves down at the table, rummaging through the cookies and potato chips. Their counselor, Ms. Ash, gave each of them a full pizza and a caffeine-filled energy drink.

The Green Machines fueled their bodies with whole-grain tuna melts with tomatoes, green peppers, and cucumbers, sprinkled with fresh mozzarella cheese. Their counselor, Elder Bean, gave each of them a vegetable salad and a **reusable water bottle**. They saved the **vegetable scraps** for composting.

The Garbage Mites hunched over after a short sprint, **huffing and puffing**. The greasy, sugary foods in their tummies made it hard to keep up.

They collapsed on the ground and found a group of worms squiggling by. One of the teammates picked up a worm and flung it across the field to be funny. The rest of the Garbage Mites laughed and then coughed. They were still out of breath.

ECO FRIENDLY

The Green Machines were warming up and running fast when they noticed the helpless worm land at their feet. Their strong bodies were well nourished by healthy foods, and they were able to stop right away to **help the worm**. They fed it the scraps they'd saved for **composting**, knowing that these would help the worm grow big and strong. "Thank you!" it cried as it hurried back to its friends.

The stadium lights flashed, and the pump-up music began playing. The crowd cheered. "To the line of scrimmage!" called President Earth.

The Green Machines' fans chanted, "Reduce! Reuse! Recycle!"

The Garbage Mites called out their own chant, "Smash it! Stash it! Trash it!" But nobody in the audience followed along.

When the game whistle blew, the Garbage Mites chuckled at the line before they hiked the ball. Then they ran, but one by one, they tripped over their own litter and fumbled the ball. The Green Machines scooped up the ball and ran into the end zone, scoring a touchdown. The game continued in this fashion until the clock ran out.

16

"The winners—and Garden Football League Champions—are the **Green Machines**! Thank you for leaving Greentopia University fresher than you found it. You are true champions!"

The crowd roared and applauded. So did the worm and all the Green Machines' new critter friends, who appreciated their **clean habitat.**

The Garbage Mites lay defeated on the field, too tired and grumpy to move. As the Green Machines paraded past, chanting, **"Reduce! Reuse! Recycle!"** they stopped to offer a hand to the Garbage Mites.

"Why are you helping us?" asked the Garbage Mites team captain.

"Because it's the right thing to do." The Green Machines team captain winked. "And besides, the key to being champions is **picking up the garbage.**"

The Garbage Mites team captain understood their mistake. "We're sorry," he said, looking around the field. "We made a mess. What can we do to fix it?"

The Green Machines team captain smiled. "Follow us, and we'll teach you everything we know!"

*** THE END

23

# Afterword

The book was inspired by the Zero Waste Football Camps that are hosted by Play Fresh for the youth. We hope to see sporting events and facilities reduce waste, reuse resources, and recycle appropriate materials. This would ultimately allow humans and nature to exist in productive harmony while fulfilling the social, economic, and personal requirements of present and future generations.

"Let's tackle the future!"

# Glossary:

a) Composting—changing waste, such as plants, vegetables, and newspapers, into healthy soil
   a) Vermicomposting—type of composting where you feed your vegetable scraps to earthworms to create valuable soil
b) Reducing—cutting back on the amount of trash we make
c) Reusing—finding a new way to use trash, so that we don't have to throw it out
d) Recycling—using trash to remake new goods that can be sold again

## Compostable Items:

Fruits/Vegetables
(i.e. Banana,
Apple, Lettuce)

Greasy Pizza and
Doughnut Cardboard box

Ice Cream Cone

Bread/Crackers

Dairy Products
(i.e. Cheese)

## Reusable Items:

BPA Free Water
Bottle

Sports Equipment

Uniforms/Clothing

Natural Resources (i.e. Wood, Water)

## Recyclable Items:

Aluminum drink cans

Plastic Milk jug

Paper Products
(i.e. Juice boxes)

# Questions for Readers

a) Which team did you root for to win the Garden Football League Championship game, and why did you root for that team?

b) If the Garbage Mites change their lifestyle, what could their new team name be? What could their coach's name be? What about their counselor? What would their uniforms look like?

c) Explain some behaviors that the Garbage Mites could learn from the Green Machines to be healthier and more successful in life.

d) How do you think the Green Machines felt when they found the injured worm? Why might they have felt that way?

e) What are five ways the Garbage Mites can improve their care of the environment?

f) Are you interested in becoming a Green Machine team captain? If so, please ask your teacher or parent/guardian to go to our website at www.playfresh.org and contact us.

9 781664 251625